The Big Wave

The Big Wave
Pearl S. Buck

HarperTrophy
A Division of HarperCollinsPublishers

Library of Congress Catalog Card Number: 48-244
ISBN 0-381-99923-8 (lib. bdg.)
Library of Congress Catalog Card Number: 85-45402
ISBN 0-06-440171-5 (pbk.)
First Harper Trophy edition, 1986.

The Big Wave

KINO

LIVED on a farm. The farm lay on the side of a mountain in Japan. The fields were terraced by walls of stone, each one of them like a broad step up the mountain. Centuries ago Kino's ancestors had built the stone walls that held up the fields.

Above all the fields stood the farmhouse that was Kino's home. Sometimes he felt the climb was a hard one, especially when he had been working in the lowest field and he wanted his supper. But after he had eaten at night and in the morning, he was glad that he lived so high up because he could look down on the broad blue ocean at the foot of the mountain.

The mountain rose so steeply out of the ocean that there was only a strip of sandy shore at its foot. Upon this strip was the small fishing village where Kino's father sold his vegetables and rice and bought his fish. From the window of his room Kino looked down upon the few thatched roofs of the village, running in two uneven lines on both sides of a cobbled street. These houses faced one another, and those that stood beside the sea did not have windows toward it. Since he enjoyed looking at the waves, Kino often wondered why the village people did not, but he never knew until he came to know Jiya, whose father was a fisherman.

Jiya lived in the last house in the row of houses toward the ocean, and his house did not have a window toward the sea either.

"Why not?" Kino asked him. "The sea is beautiful."

"The sea is our enemy," Jiya replied.

"How can you say that?" Kino asked. "Your father catches fish from the sea and sells them and that is how you live."

Jiya only shook his head. "The sea is our enemy," he repeated. "We all know it."

It was very hard to believe this. On hot sunny days, when he had finished his work, Kino ran down the path that wound through the terraces and met Jiya on the beach. They threw off their clothes and jumped into the clear sea water and swam far out toward a small island which they considered their own. Actually it belonged to an old gentleman whom they had never seen, except at a distance. Sometimes in the evening he came through the castle gate and stood looking out to sea. Then they could see him, leaning on his staff, his white beard blowing in the wind. He lived inside his castle behind a high fence of woven bamboo, on a knoll outside the village. Neither Kino or Jiya had ever been inside the gate, but sometimes when it was left open they had peeped into the garden. It was beautiful beyond anything they could imagine. Instead of grass the ground was covered with deep green moss shaded by pine trees and bamboos, and every day gardeners swept the moss with bamboo brooms until it was like a velvet carpet. They saw Old Gentleman walking under distant trees in a silver-gray robe, his hands clasped behind his back, his white head bent. He had a kind, wrinkled face, but he never saw them.

"I wonder if it is right for us to use his island without asking?" Kino asked today when they reached its beach of smooth white sand.

[5]

"He never uses it himself," Jiya replied. "Only the sacred deer live here."

The island was full of sacred deer. They were not afraid, for no one hurt them. When they saw the two boys they came to them, nuzzling into their hands for food. Sometimes Kino tied a little tin can of cakes about his waist and brought them with him to feed the deer. But he seldom had a penny, and now he reached high and picked the tender shoots of the rushes for them. The deer liked these very much and they laid their soft heads against his arm in gratitude.

Kino longed to sleep on the island some night, but Jiya was never willing. Even when they spent only the afternoon there he looked often out over the sea.

"What are you looking for?" Kino asked.

"Only to see that the ocean is not angry," Jiya replied.

Kino laughed. "Silly," he said. "The ocean cannot be angry."

"Yes, it can," Jiya insisted. "Sometimes the old ocean god begins to roll in his ocean bed and to heave up his head and shoulders, and the waves run back and forth. Then he stands upright and roars and the earth shakes under the water. I don't want to be on the island then."

"But why should he be angry with us?" Kino asked. "We are only two boys, and we never do anything to him."

"No one knows why the ocean grows angry," Jiya said anxiously.

But certainly the ocean was not angry this day. The sun sparkled deep into the clear water, and the boys swam over the silvery surface of rippling waves. Beneath them the water was miles deep. Nobody knew how deep it was, for however long the ropes that fishermen let down, weighted with iron, no bottom was ever found. Deep the water was, and the land sloped swiftly down to that fathomless ocean bed. When Kino dived, he went down—down—down, until he struck icy still water. Today when he felt the cold grasp his body he understood why Jiya was afraid, and he darted upward to the waves and the sun.

On the beach he threw himself down and was happy again, and he and Jiya searched for pebbles, blue and emerald, red and gold. They had brought little baskets woven like bags, which they had tied with string around their waists, and these they filled with the pebbles. Jiya's mother was making a pebble path in her rock garden, and nowhere were the pebbles so bright as on Deer Island.

When they were tired of the beach they went into the pine forest behind it and looked for caves. There was one cave that they always visited. They did not dare to go too deep into it, for it stretched downward and under the ocean. They knew this, and at the far end they could see the ocean filling it like a great pool and the tides rose and fell. The water was often phosphorescent and gleamed as though lamps were lighted deep beneath the surface. Once a bright fish lay dead on the rocky shore. In the dark cave it glittered in their hands, but when they ran with it into the sunshine, the colors were gone and it was gray. When they went back into the cave, it was bright again.

But however good a time they had on the island, Jiya looked often at the sun. Now he ran out on the beach and saw it sinking toward the west and he called to Kino.

"Come quickly—we must swim home."

Into the ocean, ruddy with sunset, they plunged together. The water was warm and soft and held them up, and they swam side by side across the broad channel. On the shore Jiya's father was waiting for them.

They saw him standing, his hands shading his eyes against the bright sky, looking for them. When their two black heads bobbed out of the water he shouted to them and waded out to meet them. He gave a hand to each of them, pulling them out of the white surf.

"You have never been so late before, Jiya," he said anxiously.

"We were in the cave, Father," Jiya said.

But Jiya's father held him by the shoulders. "Do not be so late," he said, and Kino, wondering, looked at him and saw that even this strong fisherman was afraid of the anger of the sea.

He bade them good night and climbed the hill to his home and found his mother ready to set the supper on the table. The food smelled delicious—hot fragrant rice, chicken soup, brown fish.

No one was worried about Kino. His father was washing himself, pouring water over his face and head with a dipper, and his little sister, Setsu, was fetching the chopsticks.

In a few minutes they were all sitting on the clean mat around a low square table, and the parents were filling the children's bowls. Nobody spoke, for it is not polite to speak until the food is served and everybody has had something to eat.

But when the supper was over and Kino's father was drinking a little hot wine out of a very small cup, and his mother was gathering together the black lacquered wood rice bowls, Kino turned to his father.

"Father, why is Jiya afraid of the ocean?" he asked.

"The ocean is very big," Kino's father replied. "Nobody knows its beginning or its end."

"Jiya's father is afraid, too," Kino said.

"We do not understand the ocean," his father said.

"I am glad we live on the land," Kino went on. "There is nothing to be afraid of on our farm."

"But one can be afraid of the land, too," his father replied. "Do you remember the great volcano we visited last autumn?"

Kino did remember. Each autumn, after the harvest was in, the family took a holiday. They always walked, even little Setsu. They carried packs of food and bedding on their backs and in their hands tall staffs to help them up the mountainsides, and then forgetting all their daily tasks they walked to some famous spot. At home a kind neighbor tended the chickens and looked after the place. Last autumn they had gone to visit a great volcano twenty miles away. Kino had never seen it before, but he had heard of it often, and sometimes on a clear day, far to the edge of the sky, if he climbed the hill behind the farm, he could see a gray, fanlike cloud. It was the smoke from the volcano, his father had told him. Sometimes the earth trembled even under the farm. That was the volcano, too.

Yes, he could remember the great yawning mouth of the volcano. He had looked down into it and he had not liked it. Great curls of yellow and black smoke were rolling about in it, and a white stream of melted rock was crawling slowly from one corner. He had wanted to go away, and even now at night sometimes when he was warm in his soft cotton quilt in his bed on the matting floor he was glad the volcano was so far away and that there were at least three mountains between.

Now he looked at his father across the low table. "Must we always be afraid of something?" he asked.

His father looked back at him. He was a strong wiry thin man and the muscles on his arms and legs were corded with hard work. His hands were rough but he kept them clean, and he always went barefoot except for straw sandals. When he came into the house, he took even these off. No one wore shoes in the house. That was how the floors kept so clean.

"We must learn to live with danger," he now said to Kino.

"Do you mean the ocean and the volcano cannot hurt us if we are not afraid?" Kino asked.

"No," his father replied. "I did not say that. Ocean is there and volcano is there. It is true that on any day ocean may rise into storm and volcano may burst into flame. We must accept this fact, but without fear. We must say, 'Someday I shall die, and does it matter whether it is by ocean or volcano, or whether I grow old and weak?'"

"I don't want to think about such things," Kino said.

"It is right for you not to think about them," his father said. "Then do not be afraid. When you are afraid, you are thinking about them all the time. Enjoy life and do not fear death—that is the way of a good Japanese."

There was much in life to enjoy. Kino had a good time every day. In the winter he went to a school in the fishing village, and he and Jiya shared a seat. They studied reading and arithmetic and all the things that other children learn in school. But in the summer Kino had to work hard on the farm, for his father needed help. Even Setsu and the mother helped when the rice seedlings had to be planted in the flooded fields on the terraces, and they helped, too, when the grain was ripe and had to be cut into sheaves and threshed. On those days Kino could not run down the mountainside to find Jiya. When the day was over he was so tired he fell asleep over his supper.

But there were days when Jiya also was too busy to play. Word came in from the fishermen up the coast that a school of fish was passing through the channels and then every fishing boat made haste to sail out of the bays and inlets into the main currents of the sea. Early in the morning, sometimes so early that the light was still that of the setting moon, Jiya and his father sailed their boat out across the silvery sea, to let down their nets at dawn. If they were lucky the nets came up so heavy with fish that it took all their strength to haul them up, and soon the bottom of the boat was flashing and sparkling with the wriggling fish.

Sometimes, if it were not seedtime or harvest, Kino went with Jiya and his father. It was an exciting thing to get up in the night and dress himself in his warm padded jacket tied around his waist. Even in summer the wind was cool over the sea at dawn. However early he got up, his mother always got up, too, and gave him a bowl of hot rice soup and some bean curd and hot tea before he started. Then she packed his lunch in a clean little wooden box, cold rice and fish and a bit of radish pickle.

Down the stone steps of the mountain path Kino ran straight to the narrow dock where the fishing boats bobbed up and down on the tide. Jiya and his father were already there, and in a few minutes the boat was nosing its way between the rocks out to the open sea. Sails set and filling with the wind, they sped straight into the dawn-lit sky. Kino crouched down on the floor behind the bow and felt his heart rise with joy and excitement. The shore fell far behind them and the boat took on the deep swell of the ocean. Soon they came to a whole fleet of fishing boats, and then together they flew after the schools of fish. It was like being a bird in a flock, flying into the sky. How exciting it was, too, to pull up the fish! At such times Kino felt Jiya was more lucky than he. Fish harvest was much easier than rice harvest.

"I wish my father were a fisherman," he would tell Jiya. "It is stupid to plow and plant and cut the sheaves, when I could just come out like this and reap fish from the sea."

Jiya shook his head. "But when the storms come, you wish yourself back upon the earth," he said. Then he laughed. "How would fish taste without rice? Think of eating only fish!"

"We need both farmers and fisherman," Jiya's father said.

On days when the sky was bright and the winds mild the ocean lay so calm and blue that it was hard to believe that it could be cruel and angry. Yet even Kino never quite forgot that under the warm blue surface the water was cold and green. When the sun shone the deep water was still. But when the deep water moved and heaved and stirred, ah, then Kino was glad that his father was a farmer and not a fisherman.

And yet, one day, it was the earth that brought the big wave. Deep under the deepest part of the ocean, miles under the still green waters, fires raged in the heart of the earth. The icy cold of the water could not chill those fires. Rocks were melted and boiled under the crust of the ocean's bed, under the weight of the water, but they could not break through. At last the steam grew so strong that it forced its way through to the mouth of the volcano. That day, as he helped his father plant turnips, Kino saw the sky overcast halfway to the zenith.

"Look, Father!" he cried. 'The volcano is burning again!"

His father stopped and gazed anxiously at the sky. "It looks very angry," he said. "I shall not sleep tonight."

All night while the others slept, Kino's father kept watch. When it was dark, the sky was lit with red and the earth trembled under the farmhouses. Down at the fishing village lights in the little houses showed that other fathers watched, too. For generations fathers had watched earth and sea.

Morning came, a strange fiery dawn. The sky was red and gray, and even here upon the farms cinders and ash fell from the volcano. Kino had a strange feeling, when he stepped barefoot upon the earth, that it was hot under his feet. In the house the mother had taken down everything from the walls that could fall or be broken, and her few good dishes she had packed into straw in a basket and set outside.

"Shall we have an earthquake, Father?" Kino asked as they ate breakfast.

"I cannot tell, my son," his father replied. "Earth and sea are struggling together against the fires inside the earth."

No fishing boats set sail that hot summer morning. There was no wind. The sea lay dead and calm, as though oil had been poured upon the waters. It was a purple gray, suave and beautiful, but when Kino looked at it he felt afraid.

"Why is the sea such a color?" he asked.

"Sea mirrors sky," his father replied. "Sea and earth and sky—if they work together against man, it will be dangerous indeed for us."

"Where are the gods at such a time?" Kino asked. "Will they not be mindful of us?"

"There are times when the gods leave man to take care of himself," his father replied. "They test us, to see how able we are to save ourselves."

"And if we are not able?" Kino asked.

"We must be able," his father replied. "Fear alone makes man weak. If you are afraid, your hands tremble, your feet falter, and your brain cannot tell hands and feet what to do."

No one stirred from home that day. Kino's father sat at the door, watching the sky and the oily sea, and

Kino stayed near him. He did not know what Jiya was doing, but he imagined that Jiya, too, stayed by his father. So the hours passed until noon.

At noon his father pointed down the mountainside. "Look at Old Gentleman's castle," he said.

Halfway down the mountainside on the knoll where the castle stood, Kino now saw a red flag rise slowly to the top of a tall pole and hang limp against the gray sky.

"Old Gentleman is telling everyone to be ready," Kino's father went on. "Twice have I seen that flag go up, both times before you were born."

"Be ready for what?" Kino asked in a frightened voice.

"For whatever happens," Kino's father replied.

At two o'clock the sky began to grow black. The air was as hot as though a forest fire were burning, but there was no sign of such a fire. The glow of the volcano glared over the mountaintop, blood-red against the black. A deep-toned bell tolled over the hills.

"What is that bell?" Kino asked his father. "I never heard it before."

"It rang twice before you were born," his father replied. "It is the bell in the temple inside the walls of

Old Gentleman's castle. He is calling the people to come up out of the village and shelter within his walls."

"Will they come?" Kino asked.

"Not all of them," his father replied. "Parents will try to make their children go, but the children will not want to leave their parents. Mothers will not want to leave fathers, and the fathers will stay by their boats. But some will want to be sure of life."

The bell kept on ringing urgently, and soon out of the village a trickling stream of people, nearly all of them children, began to climb toward the knoll.

"I wish Jiya would come," Kino said. "Do you think he will see me if I stand on the edge of the terrace and wave my white girdle cloth?"

"Try it," his father said.

"Come with me," Kino begged.

So Kino and his father stood on the edge of the terrace and waved. Kino took off the strip of white cloth from about his waist that he wore instead of a belt, and he waved it, holding it in both hands, high above his head.

Far down the hill Jiya saw the two figures and the waving strip of white against the dark sky. He was crying as he climbed, and trying not to cry. He had not wanted to leave his father, but because he was the youngest one, his older brother and his father and mother had all told him that he must go up the mountain. "We must divide ourselves," Jiya's father said. "If the ocean yields to the fires you must live after us."

"I don't want to live alone," Jiya said.

"It is your duty to obey me, as a good Japanese son," his father told him.

Jiya had run out of the house, crying. Now when he saw Kino, he decided that he would go there instead of to the castle, and he began to hurry up the hill to the farm. Next to his own family he loved Kino's strong father and kind mother. He had no sister of his own and he thought Setsu was the prettiest girl he had ever seen.

Kino's father put out his hand to help Jiya up the stone wall and Kino was just about to shout out his welcome when suddenly a hurricane wind broke out of the ocean. Kino and Jiya clung together and wrapped their arms about the father's waist.

"Look—look—what is that?" Kino screamed.

The purple rim of the ocean seemed to lift and rise against the clouds. A silver-green band of bright sky appeared like a low dawn above the sea.

"May the gods save us," Kino heard his father mutter. The castle bell began to toll again, deep and pleading. Ah, but would the people hear it in the roaring wind? Their houses had no windows toward the sea. Did they know what was about to happen?

Under the deep waters of the ocean, miles down under the cold, the earth had yielded at last to the fire. It groaned and split open and the cold water fell into the middle of the boiling rocks. Steam burst out and lifted the ocean high into the sky in a big wave. It rushed toward the shore, green and solid, frothing into white at its edges. It rose, higher and higher, lifting up hands and claws.

"I must tell my father!" Jiya screamed.

But Kino's father held him fast with both arms. "It is too late," he said sternly.

And he would not let Jiya go.

In a few seconds, before their eyes the wave had grown and come nearer and nearer, higher and higher. The air was filled with its roar and shout. It rushed over the flat still waters of the ocean and before Jiya could scream again it reached the village and covered it fathoms deep in swirling wild water, green laced with fierce white foam. The wave ran up the mountainside, until the knoll where the castle stood was an island. All who were still climbing the path were swept away— black, tossing scraps in the wicked waters. The wave ran up the mountain until Kino and Jiya saw the wavelets curl at the terrace walls upon which they stood. Then with a great sucking sigh, the wave swept back again, ebbing into the ocean, dragging everything with it, trees and stones and houses. They stood, the man and the two boys, utterly silent, clinging together, facing the wave as it went away. It swept back over the village and returned slowly again to the ocean, subsiding, sinking into a great stillness.

Upon the beach where the village stood not a house remained, no wreckage of wood or fallen stone wall, no little street of shops, no docks, not a single boat. The beach was as clean of houses as if no human beings had ever lived there. All that had been was now no more.

Jiya gave a wild cry and Kino felt him slip to the ground. He was unconscious. What he had seen was too much for him. What he knew, he could not bear. His family and his home were gone.

Kino began to cry and Kino's father did not stop him. He stooped and gathered Jiya into his arms and carried him into the house, and Kino's mother ran out of the kitchen and put down a mattress and Kino's father laid Jiya upon it.

"It is better that he is unconscious," he said gently. "Let him remain so until his own will wakes him. I will sit by him."

"I will rub his hands and feet," Kino's mother said sadly.

Kino could say nothing. He was still crying and his father let him cry for a while. Then he said to his wife:

"Heat a little rice soup for Kino and put some ginger in it. He feels cold."

Now Kino did not know until his father spoke that he did feel cold. He was shivering and he could not stop crying. Setsu came in. She had not seen the big wave, for her mother had closed the windows and drawn the curtains against the sea. But now she saw Jiya lying white-pale and still.

"Is Jiya dead?" she asked.

"No, Jiya is living," her father replied.

"Why doesn't he open his eyes?" she asked again.

"Soon he will open his eyes," the father replied.

"If Jiya is not dead, why does Kino cry?" Setsu asked.

"You are asking too many questions," her father

told her. "Go back to the kitchen and help your mother."

So Setsu went back again, sucking her forefinger, and staring at Jiya and Kino as she went, and soon the mother came in with the hot rice soup and Kino drank it. He felt warm now and he could stop crying. But he was still frightened and sad.

"What will we say to Jiya when he wakes?" he asked his father.

"We will not talk," his father replied. "We will give him warm food and let him rest. We will help him to feel he still has a home."

"Here?" Kino asked.

"Yes," his father replied. "I have always wanted another son, and Jiya will be that son. As soon as he knows that this is his home, then we must help him to understand what has happened."

So they waited for Jiya to wake.

"I don't think Jiya can ever be happy again," Kino said sorrowfully.

"Yes, he will be happy someday," his father said, "for life is always stronger than death. Jiya will feel when he wakes that he can never be happy again. He will cry and cry and we must let him cry. But he cannot always cry. After a few days he will stop crying all the time. He will cry only part of the time. He will sit sad and quiet. We must allow him to be sad and we must not make him speak. But we will do our work and live as always we do. Then one day he will be hungry and he will eat something that our mother cooks, something special, and he will begin to feel better. He will not cry any more in the daytime but only at night. We must let him cry at night. But all the time his body will be renewing itself. His blood flowing in his veins, his growing bones, his mind beginning to think again, will make him live."

"He cannot forget his father and mother and his brother!" Kino exclaimed.

"He cannot and he should not forget them," Kino's father said. "Just as he lived with them alive, he will live with them dead. Someday he will accept their death as part of his life. He will weep no more. He will carry them in his memory and his thoughts. His flesh and blood are part of them. So long as he is alive, they, too, will live in him. The big wave came, but it went away. The sun shines again, birds sing, and earth flowers. Look out over the sea now!"

Kino looked out the open door, and he saw the ocean sparkling and smooth. The sky was blue again, a few clouds on the horizon were the only sign of what had passed—except for the empty beach.

"How cruel it seems for the sky to be so clear and the ocean so calm!" Kino said.

But his father shook his head. "No, it is wonderful that after the storm the ocean grows calm, and the sky is blue once more. It was not the ocean or the sky that made the evil storm."

"Who made it?" Kino asked. He let tears roll down his cheeks, because there was so much he could not understand. But only his father saw them and his father understood.

"Ah, no one knows who makes evil storms," his father replied. "We only know that they come. When they come we must live through them as bravely as we can, and after they are gone, we must feel again how wonderful is life. Every day of life is more valuable now than it was before the storm."

"But Jiya's family—his father and mother and brother, and all the other good fisherfolk, who are lost—" Kino whispered. He could not forget the dead.

"Now we must think of Jiya," his father reminded

him. "He will open his eyes at any minute and we must be there, you to be his brother, and I to be his father. Call your mother, too, and little Setsu."

Now they heard something. Jiya's eyes were still closed, but he was sobbing in his sleep. Kino ran to fetch his mother and Setsu and they gathered about his bed, kneeling on the floor so as to be near Jiya when he opened his eyes.

In a few minutes, while they all watched, Jiya's eyelids fluttered on his pale cheeks, and then he opened his eyes. He did not know where he was. He looked from one face to the other, as though they were strangers. Then he looked up into the beams of the ceiling and around the white walls of the room. He looked at the blue-flowered quilt that covered him.

None of them said anything. They continued to kneel about him, waiting. But Setsu could not keep quiet. She clapped her hands and laughed. "Oh, Jiya has come back!" she cried. "Jiya, did you have a good dream?"

The sound of her voice made him fully awake. "My father—my mother—" he whispered.

Kino's mother took his hand. "I will be your mother now, dear Jiya," she said.

"I will be your father," Kino's father said.

"I am your brother now, Jiya," Kino faltered.

"Oh, Jiya will live with us," Setsu said joyfully.

Then Jiya understood. He got up from the bed and walked to the door that stood open to the sky and the sea. He looked down the hillside to the beach where the fishing village had stood. There was only beach, and all that remained of the twenty and more houses were a few foundation posts and some big stones. The gentle little waves of the ocean were playfully carrying the light timber that had made the houses, and throwing it on the sands and snatching it away again.

The family had followed Jiya and now they stood about him. Kino did not know what to say, for his heart ached for his friend-brother. Kino's mother was wiping her eyes, and even little Setsu looked sad. She took Jiya's hand and stroked it.

"Jiya, I will give you my pet duck," she said.

But Jiya could not speak. He kept on looking at the ocean.

"Jiya, your rice broth is growing cold," Kino's father said.

"We ought all to eat something," Kino's mother said. "I have a fine chicken for dinner."

"I'm hungry!" Setsu cried.

"Come, my son," Kino's father said to Jiya.

They persuaded him gently, gathering around him, and they entered the house again. In the pleasant cosy room they all sat down about the table.

Jiya sat with the others. He was awake, he could hear the voices of Kino's family, and he knew that Kino sat beside him. But inside he still felt asleep. He was very tired, so tired that he did not want to speak. He knew that he would never see his father and mother any more, or his brother, or the neighbors and friends of the village. He tried not to think about them or to imagine their quiet bodies, floating under the swelling waves.

"Eat, Jiya," Kino whispered. "The chicken is good."

Jiya's bowl was before him, untouched. He was not hungry. But when Kino begged him he took up his porcelain spoon and drank a little of the soup. It was hot and good, and he smelled its fragrance in his nostrils. He drank more and then he took up his chopsticks and ate some of the meat and rice. His mind was still unable to think, but his body was young and strong and glad of the food.

When they had all finished, Kino said, "Shall we go up the hillside, Jiya?"

But Jiya shook his head. "I want to go to sleep again," he said.

Kino's father understood. "Sleep is good for you," he said. And he led Jiya to his bed, and when Jiya had laid himself down he covered him with the quilt and shut the sliding panels.

"Jiya is not ready yet to live," he told Kino. "We must wait."

The body began to heal first, and Kino's father, watching Jiya tenderly, knew that the body would heal the mind and the soul. "Life is stronger than death," he told Kino again and again.

But each day Jiya was still tired. He did not want to think or to remember—he only wanted to sleep. He woke to eat and then to sleep. And when Kino's mother saw this she led him to the bedroom, and Jiya sank each time into the soft mattress spread on the floor in the quiet, clean room. He fell asleep almost at once and Kino's mother covered him and went away.

All through these days Kino did not feel like playing. He worked hard beside his father in the fields.

They did not talk much, and neither of them wanted to look at the sea. It was enough to look at the earth, dark and rich beneath their feet.

One evening, Kino climbed the hill behind the farm and looked toward the volcano. The heavy cloud of smoke had long ago gone away, and the sky was always clear now. He felt happier to know that the volcano was no longer angry, and he went down again to the house. On the threshold his father was smoking his usual evening pipe. In the house his mother was giving Setsu her evening bath.

"Is Jiya asleep already?" Kino asked his father.

"Yes, and it is a good thing for him," his father replied. "Sleep will strengthen him, and when he wakes he will be able to think and remember."

"But should he remember such sorrow?" Kino asked.

"Yes," his father replied. "Only when he dares to remember his parents will he be happy again."

They sat together, father and son, and Kino asked still another question. "Father, are we not very unfortunate people to live in Japan?"

"Why do you think so?" his father asked in reply.

"Because the volcano is behind our house and the ocean is in front, and when they work together for evil, to make the earthquake and the big wave, then we are helpless. Always many of us are lost."

"To live in the midst of danger is to know how good life is," his father replied.

"But if we are lost in the danger?" Kino asked anxiously.

"To live in the presence of death makes us brave and strong," Kino's father replied. "That is why our people never fear death. We see it too often and we do not fear it. To die a little later or a little sooner does not matter. But to live bravely, to love life, to see how beautiful the trees are and the mountains, yes, and even the sea, to enjoy work because it produces food for life —in these things we Japanese are a fortunate people. We love life because we live in danger. We do not fear death because we understand that life and death are necessary to each other."

"What is death?" Kino asked.

"Death is the great gateway," Kino's father said. His face was not at all sad. Instead, it was quiet and happy.

"The gateway—where?" Kino asked again.

Kino's father smiled. "Can you remember when you were born?"

Kino shook his head. "I was too small."

Kino's father laughed. "I remember very well. Oh, how hard you thought it was to be born! You cried and you screamed."

"Didn't I want to be born?" Kino asked. This was very interesting to him.

"You did not," his father told him smiling. "You wanted to stay just where you were in the warm, dark house of the unborn. But the time came to be born, and the gate of life opened."

"Did I know it was the gate of life?" Kino asked.

"You did not know anything about it and so you were afraid of it," his father replied. "But see how foolish you were! Here we were waiting for you, your parents, already loving you and eager to welcome you. And you have been very happy, haven't you?"

"Until the big wave came," Kino replied. "Now I am afraid again because of the death that the big wave brought."

"You are only afraid because you don't know anything about death," his father replied. "But someday you will wonder why you were afraid, even as today you wonder why you feared to be born."

While they were talking the dusk had deepened, and now coming up the mountainside they saw a flickering light. The fireflies had come out, but this light was steadily climbing the pathway toward their house.

"I wonder who comes!" Kino exclaimed.

"A visitor," his father replied. "But who can it be?"

In a few minutes they saw the visitor was Old Gentleman, coming from the castle. His manservant carried the lantern, but Old Gentleman walked behind him very sturdily, with the help of a long staff. They heard Old Gentleman's voice in the dusk.

"Is this the house of Uchiyama the farmer?" Old Gentleman asked.

"It is," his servant replied, "and the farmer sits there at his door with his son."

At this Kino's father stood up, and so did Kino.

"Please, Honored Sir," Kino's father said, "what can I do for you?"

Old Gentleman came forward. "Do you have a lad here by the name of Jiya?"

"He lies sleeping inside my house," Kino's father said.

"I wish to see him," Old Gentleman said. Anyone could see that this old gentleman was one who expected to be obeyed. But Kino's father only smiled.

"Sir, the lad is asleep and I cannot wake him. He suffered the loss of his whole family when the big wave came. Now sleep heals him."

"I will not wake him," Old Gentleman said. "I only want to see him."

So Kino's father led Old Gentleman tiptoe into the room where Jiya slept, and Kino went too. The servant held the light, shaded by his hand so it would not fall on Jiya's closed eyes. Old Gentleman looked down on the sleeping boy. Jiya was very beautiful even though so pale and weary. He was tall for his age and his body was strong, and his face showed intelligence as well as beauty.

Old Gentleman gazed at him and then motioned to the servant to lead him away. They went again to the dooryard and there Old Gentleman turned to Kino's father.

"It is my habit when the big wave comes to care for those who are orphaned. Three times the wave has come, and three times I have searched out the orphans and the widows and I have fed them and sheltered them. But I have heard of this boy Jiya and I wish to do more for him. If he is as good as he is handsome, I will make him my own son."

"But Jiya is ours!" Kino cried.

"Hush," his father cried. "We are only poor people. If Old Gentleman wants Jiya we cannot say we will not give him up."

"Exactly," Old Gentleman said. "I will educate him and give him fine clothes and send him to a good school and he may become a great man and an honor to our whole province and even to the nation."

"But if he lives in the castle we can't play together any more," Kino said.

"We must think of Jiya's good," Kino's father said. Then he turned to Old Gentleman. "Sir, it is very kind of you to propose this for Jiya. I had planned to take him for my own son, now that he has lost his birth parents, but I am only a poor farmer and I cannot pretend that my house is as good as yours, or that I can afford to send Jiya to a fine school. Tomorrow when he wakes, I will tell him of your kind offer. He will decide."

"Very well," Old Gentleman said. "But let him come and tell me himself, so that I will know how he feels."

"Certainly," Kino's father replied proudly. "Jiya will speak for himself."

How unhappy Kino now was to think that Jiya might leave this house and go and live in the castle! "If Jiya goes away, I shan't have a brother," he told his father.

"You must not be so selfish, Kino," his father replied. "You must allow Jiya to make his own choice. It would be wrong to persuade him. Kino, I forbid you to speak to Jiya of this matter. When he wakes I shall speak to him myself."

When his father was so stern Kino did not dare to disobey, and so he went sadly to bed. He thought when he drew his quilt over him that he would not sleep all night, but being young and tired he slept almost at once.

Yet as soon as he woke in the morning he remembered Jiya and the choice he had to make. He got up and washed and dressed and folded his quilt and put it into the closet where it stayed during the day. His father was already out in the field, and there Kino went and found him. It was a beautiful mild morning, and a soft mist covered the ocean so that no water could be seen.

"Is Jiya awake yet?" Kino asked his father when they had exchanged morning greetings.

"No, but he will wake soon, I think," his father

replied. He was weeding the cabbage bed carefully and Kino knelt down to help him.

"Must you tell him about Old Gentleman today?" Kino pleaded.

"I must tell him as soon as he wakes," his father replied. "It would not be fair to let Jiya grow used to thinking of this as his home. He must make the choice today, before he has time to put down his new roots."

"May I be there when you talk with him?" Kino asked next.

"No, my son," his father replied. "I shall talk to him alone and tell him all the benefits that a rich man like Old Gentleman can give him and how little we who are poor can give him."

Kino could not keep from wanting to cry. He thought his father was very hard. "But Jiya will certainly want to go away!" he sobbed.

"Then he must go," his father said.

They went into the house to have breakfast, but Kino could scarcely eat. After breakfast he went back to the field, for he did not want to play. His father stayed in the house, and he could hear Jiya getting up.

For a long time Kino stayed in the field working alone. The warm tears dropped from his eyes upon the earth, but he worked on, determined not to go to the house until he was called. Then when the sun was nearing the zenith, he heard his father's voice. He got up at once and walked along the path between the terraces until he reached the doorway. There his father stood with Jiya. Jiya's face was still pale and his eyes were red. He had been crying today, although until now he had not cried at all.

When he looked at Kino his tears began to flow again. "Jiya, you must not mind it that you cry easily," Kino's father said kindly. "Until now you could not cry because you were not fully alive. You had been hurt too much. But today you are beginning to live, and so your tears flow. It is good for you. Let your tears come and do not stop them."

Then he turned to Kino. "I have told Jiya that he must not decide until he has seen the inside of the castle. I want him to see all that Old Gentleman can give him for a home. Jiya, you know how our house is—these four rooms and the kitchen, this little farm, upon which we have to work so hard for our food. We have only what our hands can earn for us."

Kino's father held out his two hard, work-worn hands. Then he went on, "Kino, you are to go with

Jiya, and when you see the castle you must persuade him to stay there, for his own sake."

Kino heard this and felt the task laid upon him was very hard. But he only said, "I will go and wash myself, Father, and put on my good clothes."

"No," his father said. "Go as you are—you are a farmer's son."

So the two boys went down the mountainside, and avoiding the empty beach, they went to the castle. The gate was open and the garden was most beautiful. A gardener was sweeping the green moss.

When he saw them he came over to them. "What do you want?" he asked.

"My father sent us to see the honored Old Gentleman," Kino faltered.

"Are you the Uchiyama boy?" the gardener asked.

"Yes," Kino replied, "and this is Jiya, whom Old Gentleman wants to come and live here."

"Follow me, if you please," the gardener said. He bowed to Jiya and made his voice polite.

The two boys followed him along a wide, pebbled path. Over their heads the ancient pines leaned their crooked branches. In the distance beyond the forest the sun poured down upon a flower garden and a pool with a waterfall.

"How beautiful it is!" Kino whispered sadly.

Jiya did not answer. He walked along, his head held high. When they reached the house they took off their shoes and followed the gardener through a great door. Inside this the gardener paused, and a manservant came forward and asked what they wanted. The gardener whispered and the manservant nodded. "Follow me," he said to the boys.

So they followed him through wide passageways. The walls were of fine polished wood, unpainted, but smooth and silvery. Under their feet, fine woven, padded mats were softer than the moss beneath the trees. On both sides of this passageway panels slid back to show beautiful rooms, and in each room were a vase of flowers, an exquisite scroll, a few pieces of dark polished furniture. Neither Jiya nor Kino had ever seen such a house. Kino was speechless. How could he hope now that Jiya would not want to stay in the castle?

Then far in the distance they saw Old Gentleman sitting beside a small table. The table was set in front of the open sliding panels that looked into the garden, and Old Gentleman was writing. He held a brush upright in his right hand and he was carefully painting letters on a scroll, his silver-rimmed spectacles sliding down his nose.

When the two boys came near he looked up and took off his spectacles and laid down his brush. "Would you like to know what I have been writing?" he asked.

Neither Kino nor Jiya could answer. The great house, the silence, the beauty, all of this fell into place as the background for Old Gentleman himself. He was tall and thin, and his hair and beard were white. His face and hands were beautiful. The bones were delicate and the skin was smooth and brown. He looked as proud as a king, but his dark eyes were wise as an old scholar's eyes are wise.

"It is not my own poem," he said. "It is the saying of a man of India, but I like it so much that I have painted it on this scroll to hang there in the alcove where I can see it every day." He took up the scroll and read these words:

"The Children of God are very dear, but very queer—
Very nice, but very narrow."

He looked at the boys. "What do you think of it?" he said.

They looked at one another. "We do not understand it, sir," Jiya said at last. Since he was a little older than Kino, he felt he should speak.

Old Gentleman shook his head and laughed softly. "Ah, we are all the children of God," he said. Then he put on his spectacles and looked hard at Jiya. "Well?" he said. "Will you be my son?"

Jiya turned very red. He had not expected to have the question put to him so suddenly and so directly.

Old Gentleman saw he found it hard to speak. "Say yes or no," he told Jiya. "Those are not hard words to say."

"I will say,—*no!*" Jiya said. Then he felt this was harsh. "I thank you but I have a home—on the farm," he added.

Ah, how Kino felt when he heard these words! He forgot entirely about the big wave and all the sorrow it had brought, and for a moment he was filled with pure joy. Then he remembered the small farmhouse, the four little rooms and the old kitchen.

"Jiya," he said solemnly, "remember how poor we are."

Old Gentleman was smiling a half-sad little smile. "They are certainly very poor," he said to Jiya. "And here, you know, you would have everything. You can even invite this farm boy to come and play sometimes, if you like. And I am quite willing for you to give the family some money. It would be suitable, as my son, for you to help the poor."

"Where are the others who were saved from the big wave?" Jiya asked suddenly.

"Some wanted to go away, and the ones who wanted to stay are out in the back yard with my servants," Old Gentleman replied.

"Why do you not invite them to come into this big house and be your sons and daughters?" Jiya asked.

"Because I don't want them for my sons and daughters," Old Gentleman replied rather crossly. "You are a bright, handsome boy, and they told me you were the best boy in the village."

Jiya looked about him. Then he shook his head again. "I am no better than the others," he said. "My father was a fisherman."

Old Gentleman took up his spectacles and his brush again. "Very well," he said, "I will do without a son."

The manservant motioned to them and they followed, and soon they were out in the garden again.

"How foolish you are!" the manservant said to Jiya.

"Our Old Gentleman is very kind indeed. You would have everything here."

"Not everything," Jiya replied.

They went out of the gate and across the hillside again back to the farmhouse. Setsu was outside and she came running to meet them, the sleeves of her bright kimono flying behind her and her feet clattering in wooden sandals.

"Jiya has come back home!" she cried. "Jiya— Jiya—"

And Jiya, seeing her happy little face, opened his arms and gave her a great hug. For the first time he felt comfort creep into his sad heart, and this comfort came from Setsu, who was like life itself.

Their noonday meal was ready and Kino's father came in from the fields, and when he had washed they all sat down to eat.

"How happy you have made us!" he told Jiya.

"Happy indeed," Kino's mother said.

"Now I have my brother," Kino said.

Jiya only smiled. Happiness began to live in him secretly, hidden inside him, in ways he did not understand or know. The good food warmed him and his body welcomed it. Around him the love of the four people who received him glowed like a warm and welcoming fire upon the hearth.

Time passed. Jiya grew up in the farmhouse to be a tall young man, and Kino grew at his side, solid and strong, but never as tall as Jiya. Setsu grew, too, from a mischievous, laughing little girl into a gay, willful, pretty girl. But time, however long, was split in two parts by the big wave. People spoke of "the time before" and "the time after" the big wave. The big wave had changed everyone's life.

For years no one returned to live on the empty beach. The tides rose and fell, sweeping the sands clean every day. Storms came and went, but there was never again such a wave as the big one. Then people began to think that perhaps there would never again be such a big wave. The few fishermen who had listened to the tolling bell from the castle and had been saved with their wives and children had gone to other shores to fish, and they had made new fishing boats.

But as time passed after the big wave, they began to tell themselves that there was no beach quite so good as the old one. There, they said, the water was deep and great fish came close to the shore in schools. They did not need to go far out to sea to seek the booty. The channels between the islands were rich.

Now Kino and Jiya had not often gone to the beach again, either. Once or twice they had walked along the place where the street had been, and Jiya had searched for some keepsake from his home that the sea might have washed back to the shore. But nothing was ever found. The surf was too violent above deep waters, and even bodies had not returned. So the two boys, now young men, did not visit the deserted beach very often. When they went to swim in the sea, they walked across the farm and over another fold of the hill.

But Kino saw that Jiya always looked out of the door every morning and he looked at the empty beach, searching with his eyes as though something might one day come back. One day he did see something. Kino was at the door putting on his shoes and he heard Jiya cry out in a loud voice, "Kino, come here!" Quickly Kino went and Jiya pointed down the hillside. "Look— is someone building a house on the beach?"

Kino looked and saw that indeed it was so. Two men were pounding posts into the sand, and a woman and a child stood near, watching. "Can it be that they will build again on the beach?" he exclaimed.

But they could not rest with watching. They ran down the hill to the beach and went to the two men. "Are you building a house?" Jiya cried.

The men paused and the elder one nodded. "Our father used to live here and we with him. During these years we have lived in the outhouses of the castle and we have fished from other shores. Now we are tired of having no homes of our own. Besides, this is still the best of all beaches for fishing."

"But what if the big wave comes back?" Kino asked.

The men shrugged their shoulders. "There was a big wave in our great-grandfather's time. All the houses were swept away, but our grandfather came back. In our father's time the big wave came again, but now we come back."

"What of your children?" Kino asked anxiously.

"The big wave may never come back," the men said. And they began to pound the post into the sand again.

All this time Jiya had not said another word. He stood watching the work, his face musing and strange. The big wave and the sorrow it had brought had changed him forever. Never again would he laugh easily or talk carelessly. He had learned to live with his parents and his brother dead, as Kino's father had said he would, and he did not weep. He thought of them every day and he did not feel they were far from him or he from them. Their faces, their voices, the way his father talked and looked, his mother's smile, his brother's laughter, all were with him still and would be forever. But since the big wave he had been no longer a child. In school he had earnestly learned all that he could, and now he worked hard on the farm. He valued deeply everything that was good. Since the big wave had been so cruel, he could not bear cruelty, and he grew into the kindest and most gentle man that Kino had ever seen. Jiya never spoke of his loneliness. He did not want anyone to be sad because of his sadness. When he laughed at some trick of Setsu's, or when she teased him, his laughter was wonderful to hear because it was so whole and real.

Now as he stood watching the new house being made on the beach, he felt a strong delight. Could it be true that people would gather once more on this beach to make a village? Was it right that it be so?

At this moment there was a commotion on the hillside. They looked up and saw it was Old Gentleman, coming slowly down the rocky path. He was very old indeed now, and he walked with difficulty. Two menservants supported him.

The elder builder threw down his stone mallet. "Here comes our Old Gentleman," he told the others. "He is very angry or he wouldn't have left the castle."

Anyone could see that Old Gentleman was angry. He grasped his long staff, and when he came near them he pulled his beard and moved his eyebrows. His body was as thin as a bamboo, and with the wind blowing his white hair and long white beard, he looked like an ancient god out of the temple.

"You foolish children!" he cried in his high old voice. "You have left the safety of my walls and come back to this dangerous shore to make your home, as your fathers did before you. The big wave will come back and sweep you into the ocean again!"

"It may not come, Ancient Sir," the elder builder said mildly.

"It will come!" Old Gentleman insisted. "I have spent my whole life in trying to save foolish people from the big wave. But you will not be saved."

Suddenly Jiya spoke. "This is our home. Dangerous as it is, threatened by the volcano and by the sea, it is here we were born."

Old Gentleman looked at him. "Don't I know you?" he asked.

"Sir, I was once in your castle," Jiya replied.

Old Gentleman nodded. "Now I remember you. I wanted you for my son. Ah, you made a great mistake, young man! You could have lived in my castle safely forever and your children would have been safe there, too. The big wave never reaches me."

Jiya shook his head. "Your castle is not safe either," he told Old Gentleman. "If the earth shakes hard enough, your castle will crumble, too. There is no refuge for us who live on these islands. We are brave because we must be."

"Ha," the builders said, "you are right," and they went back to pounding the foundation posts.

Old Gentleman rolled his eyes a few times. "Don't ask me to save you next time the big wave comes," he told everybody.

"But you will save us," Jiya said gently, "because you are so good."

Old Gentleman shook his head at this and then smiled. "What a pity you would not be my son," he said and then he went back to the castle and shut the gates.

As for Kino and Jiya, they returned to the farmhouse, but the whole family could see that Jiya was restless from that day on. They had supposed that he would be a farmer, for he had learned everything about the land, and Kino's father trusted him with much. But Jiya fell into a mood of forgetfulness, and one day Kino's father spoke to him when they were working in the fields.

"I know that you are too good a son to be forgetful on purpose," he said. "Tell us what is on your mind."

"I want a boat," Jiya said. "I want to go back to fishing."

Kino's father was shaping a furrow. "Life is stronger than death," he said quietly.

From that day on the family knew that someday Jiya would go back to the sea, and that he would build himself a house on the beach. One after another now seven houses had risen, the frail wooden houses of fisherfolk that the big wave could lift like toys and crush and throw away. But they sheltered families, men and women and children. And again they were built with no windows toward the sea. Each family had built on the bit of land that had belonged to it before the big wave came, and at the end was left a bare piece. It belonged to Jiya now, for it had belonged once to his father.

"When I have a boat, then I shall build my own house there," Jiya said one night to the farm family.

"I shall pay you wages from this day," Kino's father said. "You have become a man."

From that day Jiya saved his wages until he had enough to buy a boat. It was a fine boat, slender and strong, of seasoned wood, and the sails were new. The day he got it he and Kino sailed it far into the channel, and Jiya had not been so happy since before the big wave. Kino could not forget the deep still cold of the bottomless waters upon which they floated. But Jiya thought only of the joy of having a boat of his own, and Kino did not want to spoil his joy by any hint of fear.

"I knew all the time that I had to come back to the sea," he told Kino.

Then to Kino's surprise Jiya grew very red. "Do you think Setsu would be afraid to live on the beach?" he asked Kino.

Kino was surprised. "Why should Setsu live on the beach?" he asked.

Jiya grew redder still, but he held his head high.

"Because that is where I shall build my home," he said firmly. "And I want Setsu to be my wife."

It was such astonishing news that Kino did not know what to say. Setsu was his little sister, and he could not believe that she was old enough to be anybody's wife. Nor, to tell the truth, could he imagine anybody wanting her for his wife. She was careless and teasing and mischievous and she still delighted to hide his things so that he could not find them.

"You would be very foolish to marry Setsu," he now told Jiya.

"I don't agree with you," Jiya said, smiling.

"But why do you want her?" Kino urged.

"Because she makes me laugh," Jiya said. "It is she who made me forget the big wave. For me—she is life."

"But she is not a good cook," Kino said. "Think how she burns the rice because she runs outside to look at something!"

"I don't mind burned rice," Jiya said, "and I will run out with her to see what she sees."

Kino said no more, but he kept looking at his friend. Jiya, wanting to build a house, to marry Setsu! He could not believe it.

When they got home he went to his father. "Do

you know that Jiya wants to marry Setsu?" he asked.

His father was looking over his seeds, for it was springtime again. "I have seen some looks pass between them," he said, smiling.

"But Jiya is too good for Setsu," Kino said.

"Setsu is very pretty," his father said.

Kino was surprised. "With that silly nose she has?"

"I believe that Jiya admires her nose," his father said calmly.

"I don't understand that," Kino replied. "Besides, she will hide his things and tease him and make him miserable."

"What makes you miserable will make him happy," his father said.

"I don't understand that, either," Kino said soberly.

"Someday you will understand," his father said, laughing. "Do you remember that I told you life is stronger than death? Jiya is ready to live."

On the day in the early summer that Jiya and Setsu were married, Kino still did not understand, for up to the very last day Setsu was naughty and mischievous, and indeed on the day of her own wedding she hid his hairbrush under his bed. "You are too silly to be married," he told her when he found it. "I feel sorry for Jiya."

Her big brown eyes laughed at him and she stuck out her small red tongue at him. "I will always be nice to Jiya," she said.

But when the wedding was over and the family took the newly married pair down the hill to the new house on the beach, Kino began to feel sad. The farmhouse would be very quiet without Setsu and he would miss her. Every day he would come to see Jiya and many times he would go fishing with him. But Setsu would not be in the farmhouse kitchen, in the rooms, or in the garden. He would miss even her teasing. He grew very grave indeed. What if the big wave came again?

There in the pretty little new house he turned to Jiya. "Jiya, what if the big wave comes again?" he asked.

"I have prepared for that," Jiya said. He led them through the little house to the room that faced the sea, the one big room in the house, where at night they would rest and where in the day they would eat and work.

All the family stood there, and as they watched, Jiya pushed back a panel in the wall. Before their eyes was the ocean, swelling and stirring under the evening wind. The sun was sinking into the water, in clouds of red and gold. They gazed out across the deep waters in silence.

"I have opened my house to the ocean," Jiya said. "If ever the big wave comes back, I shall be ready. I face it. I am not afraid."

"You are strong and brave," Kino's father said.

And they went back to the farm, and left Jiya and Setsu to make a new life in the new home on the old beach.

About the Author

PEARL S. BUCK, the famous novelist, was long involved with the lives of children. She was particularly active in work with children of Asian-American parentage, founding agencies for their adoption and for their general health, education and welfare.

America's best-loved writer about the Orient, Miss Buck lived in both China and Japan, basing many tales on her experiences in these countries. She won the Child Study Association's Children's Book Award for *The Big Wave* and the Pulitzer Prize for her novel *The Good Earth*, and in 1938 received the Nobel Prize for literature.

DATE DUE